Santa, My Neighbor

PALMETTO
PUBLISHING
Charleston, SC
www.PalmettoPublishing.com

Hardcove ISBN: 979-8-8229-3136-7
Paperback ISBN: 979-8-8229-3137-4

Santa, My Neighbor

WRITTEN BY:

Steven DeStefano

ILLUSTRATED BY:

Poornima Madhushani

Summer was over;
it was move-in day.
I loved my old house; I wanted to stay.
Some boxes were heavy,
some boxes were light.
Some couldn't be moved when
I tried with all my might.

I was on my way in
when he first caught my eye.

My new neighbor wasn't just any old guy.

I ran inside to get my book about Christmas.

I looked at the pictures to gauge the difference.

Big belly, white beard, and a little pipe...

It's him! It's him! Oh, what a sight!

But I didn't dare to tell a soul,

Not Mommy, not Daddy, not sister—he'd know!

I couldn't sleep at all that night.

"Santa's my neighbor!" It hit me like a light.

No more yelling or crying, and no sneaking food;

I have to say "please" and "thank you," no being rude.

I'll have to share, play nice, and not make a fist,

Or it's a one-way ticket to the naughty list.

Aw, man! But what if I get mad?

What if I don't listen to Mom or Dad?

I have to be a good son, brother, and student.

I have to be good; I guess I can do it.

Sister wasn't being very nice one day.

She hit me with her toy, to my dismay.

My face got red; I said, "I'll get her back!"

I picked up her doll and started to whack.

But from the corner of my eye, I saw my neighbor.

I soon dropped the doll; Santa just saved her.

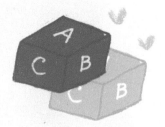

When my sister saw her doll drop to the rug,
She sighed in relief and gave me a hug.
I smiled small, so she couldn't see.
I love my sister, and she loves me.

It was time for bed one night that fall.

I wanted to stay awake, not to miss anything at all.

"Go to the bathroom, and make sure you brush."

But I wasn't sleepy and was in no rush.

"But Mommy and Daddy, why do I have to go to bed?"

"Simply because your Mommy and Daddy said."

I started to pout and flung myself to floor,

But then I remembered who lived next door.

What if he heard? I couldn't disrupt.

I stopped my crying and picked myself up.

"Sorry, Mom and Dad, I'll go to bed."
Then Daddy smiled and nodded his head.
"You can stay up for ten minutes, not one minute more.
That is your reward for acting mature."
Whew! That was close; Santa didn't hear that, maybe.
I enjoyed my ten minutes, then slept like a baby.

The bell had rung for class to start.

Time to sit at our desks, ready to get smart.

But Christmas break was right around the corner,

So when teacher yelled, students ignored her.

All the kids were screaming and running amok.

Paper planes flew, in her hair they stuck.

But there was one little boy who couldn't be heard,

Sitting in his chair, not saying a word.

I was that boy, ready to learn.

Santa's "good" list I wanted to earn.

The teacher stood up, walked over, and said,

"Thank you, young man; you're so far ahead,

And just for being such a good boy,

You may take home and keep any toy."

I was so happy for the new toy I had.

Man, being good really isn't too bad!

It was time to write a letter to Santa, I knew,
But telling a lie was now something I couldn't do.
It wasn't all the good that stood out to me.
It was the bad that Santa never did see.

Dear Santa,

Sometimes, when Mom and Dad say "no,"
I sneak a cookie and eat all the dough.
When I get new toys, and sister tries to play,
I scream and yell and turn her away.
I pretend I'm sick to stay home from school.
Sometimes, I don't listen and break every rule.
I turn on my TV when I should be asleep.
I throw temper tantrums, and I yell and weep.
I know you're my neighbor, so I've been hiding this from you:
I have done some good, but I've done some bad too.
I didn't have to be bad; it was my choice.
I hope you forgive me and still bring me toys.

I sent my letter to Santa that day.

Gee, I hoped Christmas would still go my way.

I looked out my window for the mailman to come.

Day after day, I saw my neighbor get none.

Then, one day, my neighbor did get some!

And there was one letter that got his attention.

He opened it and stood, eyes opened wide.

Santa started moving his head side to side.

He stomped his feet and clenched his fist.

"Oh no," I thought. "I won't make his list!"

Oh, the disappointment he got from that letter.

It was mine; I knew it! He'd put it right in his shredder.

Christmas was over. I started to tear.

I guess now I have to wait for next year.

On Christmas Eve,

my neighbor was nowhere to be found,

But I knew where he was. He was flying around.

All of the good kids would wake up with joy,

Sit around the tree, and play with their toys.

They'd sing Christmas songs and eat a big breakfast:

Plates full of Cinnabons and bagels, the freshest.

But not me; there will be no gifts under my tree.

Everyone's Christmas will be happier then me.

On Christmas morning, I opened my eyes
And walked into the living room. What a surprise!
There were boxes and toys and presents galore!
Even the stockings on the mantle were full!
Wrapping paper and tissues covered the ground.
I jumped on the couch and flew Superman around,
Tried on my new costumes and new superpowers,
Ate a big breakfast and sang Christmas carols.

I opened my front door to see if Santa was up.
There he was, on his lawn, drinking from a warm cup.
He looked at the sky, blue, purple, and pink;
Then he turned to me, smiled, and gave me a wink.

ABOUT THE AUTHOR

Steve DeStefano, a graduate from Rowan University, initially ventured into the world of construction, leaving behind his passion for writing. However, the birth of his children rekindled his love for storytelling. Drawing from the wellsprings of childhood wonder and parental insights, Steve crafts tales that resonate across generations. Inspired by real-life events, like a peculiar Santa-like neighbor, he weaves narratives filled with enchantment, laughter, and profound life lessons. With *Santa, My Neighbor,* Steve not only shares a magical tale but also his own journey of rediscovering the boundless realms of imagination and connection.

Milton Keynes UK
Ingram Content Group UK Ltd.
UKHW050214211123
432958UK00003B/105